Disney

Villains

Written by Melanie Zanoza

Illustrated by Art Mawhinney

Additional illustrations by the Disney Storybook Artists

Published by Louis Weber, C.E.O.
Publications International, Ltd.
7373 North Cicero Avenue, Lincolnwood, Illinois 60712
Ground Floor, 59 Gloucester Place, London W1U 8JJ

Customer Service: 1-800-595-8484
or customer_service@pilbooks.com

www.pilbooks.com

Manufactured in China.

p i kids is a registered trademark of Publications International, Ltd.
Look and Find is a registered trademark of Publications International, Ltd.,
in the United States and in Canada.

8 7 6 5 4 3 2 1

ISBN-13: 978-1-4127-7694-3
ISBN-10: 1-4127-7694-5

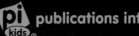

publications international, ltd.

While Peter Pan battles Captain Hook high atop the Jolly Roger, hit the decks and look for these prized pirate possessions.

Silver goblet

Treasure chest

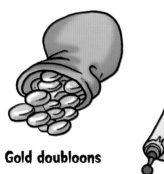

Gold doubloons

Treasure map

Parrot

Eye patch

Jewels

The Queen is preparing to disguise herself as a peddler woman to trick Snow White. Look around her dungeon lab for these things she will need to complete the transformation.

Old Hag's Cackle

Black of Night

Mummy Dust

Scream of Fright

Cloak

Basket of apples

Scar has tricked Simba into visiting the elephant graveyard, where he hopes his hyenas will teach the cub a lesson. Help Simba and Nala through the maze of bones to escape the mean animals.

Gaston is upset that Belle won't marry him, but there are plenty of other villagers enamored with him. Can you find these admiring acquaintances?

LeFou

Tom

Dick

Monsieur Chat

Stanley

Madame Nouveau-Riche

Mademoiselle Rouge

Jafar was just about to hypnotize the Sultan when Prince Ali Ababwa showed up. If Jasmine falls for him, Jafar will never be Sultan. While Jafar tries to get rid of the new suitor, look for these members of Prince Ali's entrance parade.

This scarf dancer

Purple peacock

Lion

White Persian monkey

Golden camel statue

This flag carrier

Bear

Cruella De Vil has brought 99 Dalmatian puppies to her decrepit mansion. As she discusses her evil plans with Jasper and Horace, see if you can spot these familiar puppies in the crowd.

Freckles

Lucky

Patch

Penny

Pepper

Rolly

Ursula the sea witch is about to give Ariel legs in exchange for her voice. Swim around Ursula's lair and look for these bottles the witch will need to cast her terrible spell.

The entire kingdom has gathered to see the baby princess, Aurora. But one person didn't make the guest list. As the evil fairy Maleficent takes her revenge, look around the celebration for these frightened guests.

Captain Hook was afraid of the Crocodile, which he could always hear coming because of the clock it had swallowed. With a pinch of pixie dust, fly back to the ship and look for these timepieces there.

Wristwatch

Alarm clock

Pocket watch

Grandfather clock

Hourglass

Sundial

The Queen keeps some handy items in her laboratory. Can you spot these books she finds especially useful?

Black Magic

Alchemy

Sorcery

Black Arts

Witch Craft

Poisons

Simba and Nala thought the elephant graveyard would be an exciting place to play. In fact, some of the bones there look extra fun — can you spot these?

Straight slide

Teeter-totter

Monkey bars

Swing

Merry-go-round

Curvy slide

Tree house

Head back to the lodge and look for these items that help Gaston keep looking so handsome.

Brush

Nail file

Mirror

Hand weights

Boot polish

Five dozen eggs

Jafar uses his snake-shaped staff to cast his spells. Slither back to the Sultan's palace and look for these real snakes there.

Tiptoe back into Cruella's manor and look for these other spotted things there.

Lamp shade

Hat

Cup

Ladybug toy

Cake

Shoe

Curtain

Ursula treasures the souls she has collected. Dive back into her lair and look for these items that only Ariel treasures.

Snarfblatt

Dinglehopper

Whatzit

Whozit

Gadgets and gizmos

Thingamabob

Statue of Prince Eric

Baby Aurora has received many presents today. Fly back to the castle and look for these special gifts any girl would be lucky to have.

Gift of Beauty

Gift of Song

Gift of Dance

Gift of Intelligence

Gift of Painting

Gift of Curiosity